My Vulva

Written and illustrated by Courtney J. Angermeier

To the students, parents and friends who helped me develop this book. May you be safe, healthy, and happy.

-cja

My Vulva

I have a vulva,
and I am
PROUD OF IT.

Some people don't have vulvas.

Before I knew better,

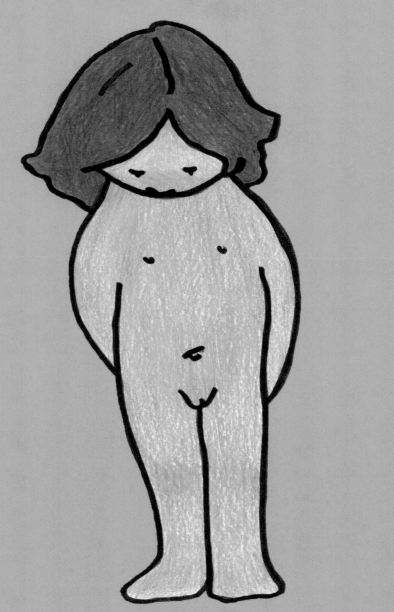

Looking down at it,
it looked like a bottom.

I said, "I have two bottoms.

One in front

and one in back"

My dad said the one in front wasn't a bottom.

It was a VULVA.

My mom said my vulva
was very special.

I take care of
my special vulva.

I wash it.

I wipe it.

Sometimes I give it a pat
and say, "good vulva."

NO ONE can
touch my vulva
unless I say so.

It is MINE.

My vulva
is where
my pee
comes out.

My vulva
is where,
when I
grow up, a
baby can
come out.

Mom says there's a hole.

Dad says people all over

the world

have vulvas.

YAY
VULVAS!

I have a vulva...

and I LOVE it!

Note to Grownups:

Discussing bodies and sex (biological sex, sexuality, sexual orientation, gender identity and gender expression) with you child can be SUPER daunting. Many of us were brought up with little or no information about, let alone pride in our own bodies. We want to encourage the development of agency, curiosity, knowledge, and delight in our children with regard to their own bodies, but it can be difficult at times to know how to support that development. One way is to start early.

Children are generally fascinated with bodies. Between the ages of two and six, they want to touch and name everything. They want to talk about them. They want to see where the pee comes out. They start asking questions about reproduction, sexual function, and gender.

All of these normal developmental stages can be supported by our enthusiasm, honesty and sensitivity. We can celebrate with our children as they discover their own bodies. We can also let them know the right times, places, and situations to engage in that discovery. We can listen carefully to our children's questions and be on the lookout for "teachable moments". Simple, honest answers and explanations work best. Give one piece of information at a time and, when your child sees that you are open and comfortable talking, they will ask more questions and share their experiences as they need to…both when they are small and as they grow.

I wrote this book in response to a variety of experiences I had as a preschool teacher in a classroom of three to five-year-olds. I noticed that while children with penises were pretty excited to talk about that body part, children with vulvas often struggled even to name their body parts. I did a study of available books that talked about bodies and body autonomy, and found some pretty glaring gaps in the literature. I wanted to fill some that gap, but found it could not be done all in one book. For example, not everyone with a vulva identifies as female (and not every female has a vulva). I struggled to make this book inclusive without being too complicated. It has flaws, but that issue is something that you can definitely talk to your child about in reading and re-reading. Similarly, this child is having conversations about her body with her mother and father, as I wanted to empower grownups of both genders to talk to their children about these issues. This too will not necessarily be the setup of your family, and I encourage you to adapt the text to suit and/or to address that the variety of caretaker identities in our rich world. Also, while the child in this book is light-skinned and able-bodied, of course not everyone is, and these are indeed aspects of our bodies that I encourage grownups to address with kids.

It is important too that we as adults continue to learn about and celebrate our own bodies, educate ourselves about consent and coercion, and to examine the places that this book and our conversations about it are asking us to grow. In many ways, this book grew out of my own discomfort. As I researched it, I talked to many wonderful parents, educators, and healthcare professionals. Many of them shared their own experiences of sorrow, contempt, and confusion regarding their own bodies; not having the words to talk about their own bodies, not having safe or supportive space in which to ask questions or gain appropriate information, not having a sense of agency with regard to their physical person, and/or not being able to celebrate or love their own bodies. Addressing these issues for ourselves too is an important piece of supporting our children.

I wish you the best in all of it.

I have included a diagram below for the purpose of clarity and a short list of resources for wherever it is this might take you next:

It's Not the Stork by Robie Harris
The Family Book by Todd Parr
What Makes a Baby by Cory Silverberg
It Feels Good to Be Yourself by Theresa Thorn
Videos at *AMAZE Junior*: https://amaze.org/jr/

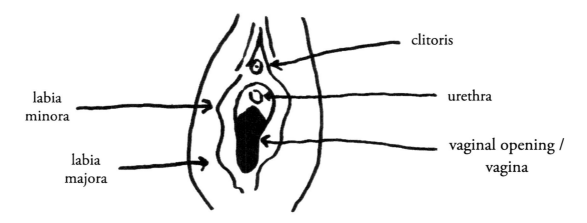

*Yes, the vagina is *one part* of the vulva. The vulva is the proper name for the female genitalia in toto.

Dr. Courtney J. Angermeier is a professor, teacher and graphic novelist living in Albuquerque, New Mexico. She teaches Sex Education to high school students and works with pre-service teachers in the College of Education at the University of New Mexico.

Made in the USA
Middletown, DE
17 November 2021